# THE GHOSTED SERVANT

*A Journey Through Haunted History*

**Solomon G. Adegboye**

## THE GHOSTED SERVANT     1

*A Journey Through Haunted History*     1

Introduction     5

Chapter One     8

The Arrival     8

Chapter Two     15

The Historical Background of the Mansion     15

Chapter Three     21

Encounter with the Spectre     21

Chapter Four     28

The Revelation Emerges     28

Chapter Five     35

The Housemaid Background  A History of Difficulties     35

Chapter Six     40

Ghost's Previous Existence     40

Chapter Seven     46

Allies and Adversaries     46

Chapter Eight     52

The Haunting Intensifies     52

Chapter Nine     58

Discovering The Truth     58

Chapter Ten     64

The Ghost Request     64

Communicating with the Ghost     64

Chapter Eleven     70

The Supernatural Ally     70

Chapter Twelve                                          76

   The Final Puzzle                                 76

Chapter Thirteen                                        82

   The Climax                                      82

Chapter Fourteen                                        88

   Aftermath                                       88

Chapter Fifteen                                         94

   A New Beginning                                 94

# Introduction

Downhill is an impressive structure situated on the outskirts of a little settlement shrouded in mist. It functions as a vigilant protector, representing a bygone era. The mansion has been shrouded in mystery and stories of the supernatural, persisting across numerous generations. The populace holds it in high esteem and fear, sharing tales of ghostly apparitions and unexplainable events.

Victoria John, a youthful domestic worker seeking a fresh start, is curiously drawn to this enigmatic property. Victoria, burdened by her personal past and yearning for a feeling of acceptance, expects that Down Hill will offer her solace and stability. Without her knowledge, her arrival will awaken inactive spirits and set in motion a series of events that will profoundly change her life.

As soon as Victoria steps into the estate, she instantly senses the overpowering atmosphere and the unseen scrutiny monitoring her every move. The expansive foyer exudes both visual elegance and a spooky ambiance of unknown stories, with its grand staircase and antique furnishings. Both the remaining staff members and residents are equally intriguing, each of them harbouring their own private secrets and fears.

As Victoria familiarises herself with her role, she begins to experience unusual occurrences—objects being moved without any discernible reason, faint whispers throughout the late hours of the night, and fleeting glimpses of spectral figures. Motivated by her curiosity and empathy, she began a comprehensive investigation into the mansion's history, uncovering stories of love, betrayal, and sadness that have deeply shaped the soul of Ravenswood.

Victoria, motivated by the ghostly presence of Lois, a once-respected servant whose untimely death has bound her spirit to the estate, embarks on a mission to unravel the mysteries that imprison the souls within Ravenswood. Throughout her expedition, she discovers hidden chambers, ancient manuscripts, and clues that indicate the existence of a malicious entity. Her encounters with kind and malevolent spirits test her courage and resolve, motivating her to confront her internal conflicts.

"The Ghosted Servant" is not just a story about supernatural events and encounters with ghosts; it is a story about finding atonement, the interconnectedness of all things, and the enduring strength of the human spirit. While exploring the line between life and death, Victoria realizes that the past is always there and that the future holds the possibility of healing and hope.

Through the contents of this book, you will join Victoria on her journey through the eerie hallways of Down Hill, uncovering concealed realities and establishing relationships with invisible beings. Prepare to be captivated by a story in which the last traces of the past have a strong impact on the present, and where the courage to confront one's fears can lead to unexpected and profound transformations.

Hello and welcome to Down Hill. The ethereal beings are in a condition of eager expectation.

# Chapter One

## The Arrival

Victoria John arrived at the gates of Downhill on a chilly autumn morning. The towering iron gates stood prominently, embellished with elaborate motifs that appeared to narrate tales of bygone eras. Victoria, a lady in her mid-twenties, became a housemaid at the mansion due to a string of tragic events that left her in urgent need of a job. Before entering, she straightened her coat and inhaled deeply, causing the sound of the gates opening to reverberate in the quiet atmosphere.

Downhill was situated on a vast estate, with its magnificent architecture serving as a reminder of a bygone period. The home was renowned in the neighboring community; stories of its magnificence were only equaled by rumors of its supernatural presence. Victoria was aware of the stories, but she was not easily influenced by supernatural myths. She required the employment opportunity, and the remuneration was satisfactory.

As she neared the colossal entrance, the doors effortlessly swung open. Waiting to welcome her was Mrs. Thompson, the strict housekeeper who managed the family with strict discipline. The woman's hair, already showing signs of grey, was tightly pushed back into a bun. Her intense blue eyes carefully examined Victoria's appearance from top to bottom.

"Are you Miss John?" Mrs. Thompson's speech possessed the same level of sharpness as her stare.

"Certainly, madam," Victoria responded, endeavoring to project assurance.

"Please accompany me." "I will escort you to your assigned living quarters and provide you with a detailed explanation of your responsibilities." Mrs. Thompson swiftly pivoted and guided Victoria across the impressive entrance hall, her footfall resounding in the vast expanse.

Initial Observations

Victoria's initial perception of the home was a combination of astonishment and discomfort. The entryway was vast, featuring a lofty ceiling embellished with a splendid chandelier that shimmered despite the accumulation of dust. The walls were adorned with images of austere ancestors, whose gaze appeared to track her every step. The atmosphere was laden with the aroma of aged timber and a subtle, almost delicate, sweetness reminiscent of wilting blossoms.

Mrs. Thompson guided her into a lengthy corridor, where the wooden flooring emitted a creaking sound beneath their feet. They encountered other sealed doors, prompting Victoria to ponder about the contents concealed behind them. The mansion exuded a palpable aura, as if it possessed a sentient consciousness that acknowledged her existence.

"Your room is located at the far end of this corridor," Mrs. Thompson stated, as she opened a door leading to a compact yet well-maintained room. "You will commence your responsibilities promptly at 6 a.m." The morning meal is provided at 5:30 in the living quarters designated for the staff. Ensure punctuality and avoid tardiness.

Victoria acknowledged, absorbing her unfamiliar environment. The room was unadorned, furnished with only a solitary bed, a dresser, and a petite window that provided a view of the neglected gardens. The item was simple, but it would be adequate.

"Additionally," Mrs. Thompson said, her tone becoming increasingly grave. "Certain areas of this house are restricted." Under no circumstances should you explore the eastern wing, regardless of any sounds you may hear. Is my message comprehensible?

"Certainly, madam," Victoria responded, feeling a chill travel over her back.

Having said that, Mrs. Thompson departed, firmly shutting the door behind her with a resolute click. Victoria perched on the edge of her bed, her thoughts whirling. What might be present in the east wing that justified such a stringent cautionary notice?

Unusual Occurrences

Victoria's initial days at Down hill were filled with a flurry of commotion. She rapidly acquired proficiency in her responsibilities, which encompassed tasks such as tidying, laundering, and assisting with dinner arrangements. The remaining staff members exhibited politeness but maintained a reserved demeanor, preferring alone and refraining from engaging in superfluous dialogue.

Victoria soon began to observe peculiar occurrences within the mansion. The series of events commenced with minor occurrences: a door that she had securely shut was discovered slightly open, murmurs in the corridors while no other individuals were present, and chilly gusts of air in rooms devoid of any open windows. She constantly had a persistent sense of surveillance, even alone.

While she was cleaning the drawing room, she suddenly experienced a significant drop in temperature. As she rotated, she observed a silhouette swiftly move over the distant wall. She hurried to the location, but it was devoid of any individuals. Her cardiac muscles throbbed vigorously within her thoracic cavity as she endeavored to persuade herself that it was merely a figment of her mind.

During another evening, Victoria was roused from her

sleep by the sound of gentle weeping. She elevated her position on the bed, exerting effort to discern the source of the sound. The auditory stimulus appeared to originate from the corridor. She enveloped herself in her robe and unlocked the door, cautiously gazing into the poorly illuminated hallway. The persistent weeping compelled her to venture towards the prohibited east wing. Recalling Mrs. Thompson's caution, she momentarily paused, but her inquisitiveness overpowered her.

Upon nearing the entrance to the east wing, the sobbing immediately ceased. Victoria remained stationary, her hand suspended in mid-air, just above the doorknob. She experienced a chilling gust of wind and perceived a faint murmur, as though someone was directly behind her. She rotated swiftly, but the corridor was devoid of anybody. Her bravery wavered, causing her to withdraw to her room and firmly shut the door.

Victoria reclined on her bed, experiencing insomnia while her thoughts raced with inquiries. What events were occurring within the confines of this residence? What was the restricted content in the east wing?

Over time, the unusual occurrences grew in both frequency and intensity. Victoria was aware of the necessity to seek answers, while also understanding the importance of exercising caution. The Downhill was a clandestine location, and she was resolute in her determination to unveil its hidden truths, regardless of the consequences.

## Chapter Two

## The Historical Background of the Mansion

Downhill exemplified a past era, showcasing a combination of Gothic Revival and Victorian architectural styles. The home, built in the late 1800s, was conceived by the esteemed architect, Sir Reginald Whitaker, known for his famed designs characterized by precise detail and grandeur. The mansion was commissioned by Lord Henry Ravenswood, a prosperous manufacturer, to create a residence that would accurately represent his substantial wealth and social standing.

The mansion's exterior showcased exquisite craftsmanship. The outside was constructed using dark grey stone, which imparted a menacing and almost ominous look to the building. The windows were embellished with stained glass panels showing different scenes from the Ravenswood family's history and were surrounded by tall, pointed arches. The gargoyles were positioned on the corners of the roof, their monstrous visages providing a striking juxtaposition to the otherwise elegant style.

The interior of the home was similarly remarkable. The large foyer, adorned with a majestic staircase and elegant marble floors, establishes the ambiance that will be maintained throughout the entire house. The high ceilings were upheld by elaborately carved wooden beams, while crystal chandeliers adorned nearly every room, emitting a cozy and radiant golden light. The walls were adorned with opulent tapestries and paintings, each depicting the family's ancestry and achievements.

The library was an extraordinary sight, including towering bookshelves loaded with scarce and antiquated volumes. A helical staircase ascended to a mezzanine level, revealing more volumes and concealed alcoves for reading. The ballroom, characterized by its spaciousness and sophisticated furnishings, had been a venue for numerous extravagant celebrations during its prime, resonating with the melodies and merriment that now remain absent within its quiet corridors.

Previous residents

The Ravenswood family has a lengthy and illustrious history, with its wealth derived from the triumphs of their diverse economic endeavors. Lord Henry Ravenswood, the initial proprietor, was renowned for his astute commercial acumen and relentless quest for riches. Lady Juliet Ravenswood, the wife of the individual in question, was widely recognized for her exceptional physical attractiveness and her active participation in philanthropic endeavors and extravagant social gatherings.

Nevertheless, misfortune appeared to consistently accompany the Ravenswood family throughout their history. Edward, the son of Lord Henry, became the owner of the mansion following his father's premature demise, which occurred in a perplexing manner. Edward, in contrast to his father, had qualities of kindness and generosity, which endeared him to the local community. Nevertheless, his time in the estate was overshadowed by personal tragedies. Lois, his spouse, passed away while giving birth, and their sole offspring, Thomas, vanished without any evidence when he was 10 years old.

Over time, the ownership of the mansion was transferred multiple times. Every subsequent owner appeared to contribute to its ominous past. Accounts of abrupt fatalities, vanishings, and peculiar incidents circulated, causing several residents to descend into insanity. Before its current state of decay, the property was owned by a secluded millionaire called Jonathan Pemberton, who was discovered deceased in the library, his face displaying an unmistakable expression of extreme dread.

Ghostly Whispers

The residents whispered about Downhill in subdued voices, their tones tinged with a blend of trepidation and intrigue. Tales of apparitions and paranormal phenomena were prevalent, and the estate had gained a firmly established notoriety as a haunted dwelling.

One enduring myth revolved around the figure of Lady Juliet Ravenswood. According to legend, her apparition was rumored to appear in the gardens during evenings illuminated by the moon, with her luminous white attire standing out in the dark. Several individuals asserted that they had perceived her melancholic wails, which served as a poignant reminder of her terrible history.

The vanishing of young Thomas Ravenswood contributed to the mansion's aura of mystery. There was a widespread belief that his ghost continued to wander the corridors, seeking a means to break free from the boundaries of the mansion. The children in the village would challenge one another to trespass onto the premises and attempt to catch sight of the spectral lad, although none dared to remain for an extended period.

The death of Jonathan Pemberton served to intensify the rumors. Individuals who had entered the residence shortly after his death reported experiencing areas of unusually low temperature, lights that were intermittently dimming and brightening, and things that were in motion without any apparent cause. The most eerie account was an apparition observed in the library, with its visage twisted in the exact same expression of fear as Pemberton's upon discovery.

The mansion's unsettling notoriety, there were consistently individuals intrigued enough to investigate its enigmas. Paranormal investigators, individuals seeking excitement, and scholars alike have all endeavored to unveil the veracity underlying supernatural phenomena. Several individuals departed with accounts of their peculiar encounters, while certain individuals declined to discuss the sights they had witnessed.

As Victoria explored the history of Downhill more extensively, she couldn't help but experience an increasing sense of affinity towards the location. The tales of bygone eras, the intricate design of the building, and the faint echoes of spirits all conspired to captivate her, drawing her deeper into the mysterious allure of the home. She recognized that comprehending the historical background was crucial for deciphering the enigmas that plagued the mansion, and she was resolute in her determination to reveal the truth, regardless of its potential consequences.

## Chapter Three

### Encounter with the Spectre

During the late hours of one night, Victoria John experienced her initial direct encounter with the apparition of Downhill. The remaining members of the household had already gone to bed, and the mansion was enveloped in an almost suffocating stillness. Victoria was assigned the responsibility of cleaning the library, a space that simultaneously intrigued and frightened her. The faint illumination emitted by the oil lamp created elongated, unsteady shadows that stretched over the rows of aged books and dirty shelves.

While cleaning a tall shelf, she sensed a chilling gust of wind caress her neck. She turned, anticipating an open window, but all of them were firmly closed. The room's temperature noticeably decreased, causing her breath to form a mist in the frigid air. Abruptly, the lamp flickered and extinguished, enveloping the room in darkness.

She felt a sudden sensation of coldness as she struggled to find matches to reignite the lamp. Amidst the complete darkness, she perceived a faint murmur, barely discernible, akin to the gentle rustling of leaves on a blustery evening. She made an effort to listen intently, feeling her heart beat rapidly in her chest. The murmur intensified, becoming more discernible until she could distinguish a solitary utterance: "Victoria..."

The voice was unfamiliar to her, yet it had a profound impact on her. With hands trembling, she ignited the lamp, causing the flame to flicker and create a small illuminated area. Upon acclimating her vision, she perceived a silhouette positioned at the furthest extremity of the chamber.

The apparition appeared translucent, with its shape shimmering in the dim illumination. The individual in question was a female, attired in a vintage outfit, with her hair cascading down her shoulders. Victoria's eyes exuded a profound melancholy, carrying a timeless grief that penetrated her soul. The apparition extended its hand towards her, as if attempting to make contact, then promptly disappeared as abruptly as it had materialised, leaving Victoria in solitude and deeply unsettled.

Characteristics of Ghosts

The spectral presence of Downhill was unlike any apparition that Victoria had ever conceived. She had an otherworldly and hauntingly lovely countenance. The gown she wore was a relic of a past era, adorned with intricate lace and crafted from exquisite fabric that appeared to effortlessly glide around her. The woman had black, wavy hair that framed her face. Her face appeared youthful yet timeless, and her eyes conveyed a profound sense of emotion and a rich past.

Victoria was especially impressed by the ghost's demeanor. She appeared neither evil nor malicious, but simply disoriented and filled with despair. She moved with a methodical and unhurried pace as if she were trapped in a constant state of yearning. The apparition had a clear attraction to specific sections of the mansion, specifically the library and the east wing, where it manifested with the highest frequency.

Encounters with the ghost were brief and frequently understated. Victoria would perceive a chilling draft, discern a faint murmur, or notice the apparition from the periphery of her vision. Occasionally, the apparition would manipulate objects with a delicate touch, seemingly attempting to convey a message or attract notice towards a particular matter. Books would spontaneously dislodge from shelves, doors would autonomously open, and candles would intermittently flicker without any discernible reason.

Notwithstanding the unsettling quality of these events, Victoria perceived no danger emanating from the apparition. However, she experienced a profound and unexplainable sense of empathy towards the spirit. The spirit seemed to be attempting to communicate with her, eager to reveal a long-neglected narrative.

Implicit Norms

As Victoria persisted in perceiving the ghost's existence, she gradually identified a series of implicit guidelines that the ghost appeared to adhere to within the estate. Initially, these principles were not readily apparent, but gradually, discernible patterns surfaced that provided Victoria with a deeper understanding of the ghost's actions.

Initially, the ghost refrained from venturing outside the confines of the mansion. Despite her restless spirit, she was restricted within the boundaries of Downhill. This indicated a profound emotional connection to the house, possibly because of significant experiences or memories that kept her strongly connected to the location.

The apparition exhibited heightened activity during specific periods of both day and night. Victoria frequently detected the ghost's presence during late evenings and early mornings. This correlation may be attributed to the instances when big occurrences took place in the ghost's history, although Victoria could only make educated guesses.

The apparition appeared to deliberately steer clear of several regions within the estate, including the servants' quarters and the kitchens. Victoria pondered whether the live folks were being respected or whether there was something about certain regions that repelled the ghost. Finally, the ghost consistently engaged with Victoria and other staff members in a kind manner. She was consistently nonviolent and had no signs of aggressiveness. She seemed to be constrained by a set of rules, fully conscious of her existence as a spirit and the limitations that accompanied it.

While contemplating these implicit guidelines, Victoria experienced an increasing resolve to comprehend the narrative of the ghost. There was an unresolved matter, a perplexing enigma that required resolution. Victoria was aware that unravelling the deeper enigmas of Down hill hinged on learning the truth about the ghost, who had a significant role in the mansion's past. With every meeting,

Victoria's determination became stronger, and she readied herself for the upcoming expedition, fully prepared to confront any enigmas that the apparition and the manor concealed.

## Chapter Four

### The Revelation Emerges

Over time, Victoria started to observe inconspicuous indications and signals that suggested a more profound enigma surrounding the apparition of Downhill. The sequence of events commenced with minuscule, apparently inconsequential particulars that progressively assembled into a more comprehensive enigma.

During her routine dusting of the library shelves, Victoria discovered an antiquated, leather-bound notebook hidden behind a queue of books. The journal was owned by Edward Ravenswood, and its pages were filled with precise entries documenting his life, romantic relationships, and personal tragedies. One specific entry captured her attention. Edward expressed profound grief at the passing of his spouse, Lois, and the enigmatic vanishing of their child, Thomas. He recounted peculiar incidents at the mansion, detailing a persistent sensation of being observed, especially in the east wing.

Victoria discovered an ancient locket in a neglected drawer in the drawing room, providing another piece of evidence.

Contained within the locket was a little depiction of a youthful lady, whom Victoria identified as the apparition she had previously encountered. The reverse side of the locket bore the etched initials "E.R." along with the precise date of October 15, 1892. This revelation substantiated the fact that the apparition was, without a doubt, Juliet Ravenswood, the spouse of Edward.

Additionally, Victoria discovered a collection of correspondence concealed in the attic, secured with a weathered ribbon. Edward penned the letters to his spouse during their romantic relationship. Their conversation revolved around eternal love and a commitment to safeguard their family at any expense. Nevertheless, the recent correspondence alluded to an escalating apprehension and an intangible menace lurking within the estate. These correspondences heightened Victoria's comprehension of the specter's grief and her lingering torment.

**Interactions with the Personnel**

With a strong will to acquire more knowledge, Victoria initiated a covert inquiry among her colleagues to gather information about their encounters and expertise regarding the apparition. The majority of individuals were hesitant to talk, as they were afraid of facing punishment or being mocked. However, a small number of people were willing to tell their narratives.

The housekeeper, Mrs. Thompson, was the first to begin her duties. With a tenure of more than three decades at the estate, she had observed innumerable peculiar incidents. She mentioned areas of low temperature, voices without physical presence, and the sensation of being observed. Mrs. Thompson verified that the eastern section has consistently instilled dread and intrigue. A significant number of the former employees declined to explore the location, alleging that it was haunted by the apparitions of the Ravenswood family.

Additionally, Mr. Collins, the elderly horticulturist, possessed his own anecdotes. He had observed the silhouette of a female in the grounds throughout the late hours of the night, consistently in close proximity to the ancient fountain that was presently enveloped in ivy. He had the belief that the apparition was the spectral manifestation of Juliet, inexplicably attracted to the exact location where she often passed her leisure hours. Mr. Collins recollected the sound of her voice on multiple occasions, gently beckoning for her missing kid.

Even the youthful Sarah, who worked as a scullery maid, had her own experiences. Frequently, she would perceive the auditory manifestation of a child's mirth emanating from the eastern section of the building, subsequently accompanied by an intense feeling of profound sorrow. Sarah had the belief that Thomas's spirit remained confined within the house, unable to progress further.

These interactions validated Victoria's thoughts that the ghost's existence was connected to unsolved matters from her past. The accounts offered by the crew yielded useful insights and served as a source of motivation for Victoria to persist in her investigation.

Concealed Chambers

Driven by her inquisitiveness, Victoria meticulously investigated the estate, diligently searching for concealed chambers and covert corridors that could perhaps contain additional evidence. She commenced her investigation by examining a meticulously crafted blueprint of the grand estate that she stumbled upon in the library. The aged map displayed other chambers and corridors that were not well recognized.

The initial revelation she made was the existence of a compact chamber concealed beneath a bookcase within the library. She discovered a mechanism that, when triggered, unveiled a slender stairway descending into a concealed compartment. The chamber housed antiquated furniture enveloped in a layer of dust, as well as multiple trunks brimming with personal possessions. Included in the collection were a series of keys, each marked with a distinct area of the residence.

Victoria utilized the keys to open a door located in the eastern section of the building, which granted access to a nursery that had been neglected and abandoned for a considerable period. The room appeared to be suspended in time, with toys strewn across the floor and a rocking chair swaying softly, as if it had been just disturbed. An image of a youthful Thomas was displayed on the wall, with his pure countenance radiating a smile towards her. Victoria experienced a surge of melancholy and resolve to unveil the truth regarding his vanishing.

Victoria discovered an underground cellar through yet another concealed entrance. The cellar exuded moisture and obscurity, brimming with antiquated wine barrels and crates. Within a specific location, she discovered a securely fastened container. With the aid of a single key, she unlocked the object, exposing a compilation of letters and documents that meticulously chronicled a sequence of sinister occurrences entangling the Ravenswood lineage. The documents contained information regarding clandestine ceremonies and a time-honored curse that afflicted the family throughout many successive generations.

Upon analyzing these indications, Victoria discerned that the ghost's anguish sprang not only from individual bereavement but also from a profound and ominous past associated with the Ravenswood lineage. The concealed chambers and corridors she uncovered yielded not just tangible proof, but also a route to comprehending the specter's torment and the sorrowful occurrences that tethered her to the manor.

With every subsequent revelation, the enigma of Downhill unravelled more, exposing intricate layers of hidden truths and an eerie heritage that required comprehension. Victoria was aware that she was on the verge of revealing the truth, which could maybe lead to finding a solution to calm the unsettled spirits in the house.

## Chapter Five

## The Housemaid Background

## A History of Difficulties

Victoria John's journey to Downhill was fraught with complexity. Victoria's early years were marked by a series of challenges, as she grew up in a modest household in a rural village. Victoria's father, a kind yet economically disadvantaged artist, passed away when she was merely 10 years old, leaving her mother with the responsibility of caring for Victoria and her two younger brothers. The user's mother, a diligent seamstress, made tremendous efforts to cover all bills, but the unrelenting financial load proved insurmountable.

Victoria's adolescence was marred by further misfortune. When Victoria was sixteen years old, her mother was extremely ill and passed away, leaving Victoria with the responsibility of taking care of her siblings. Victoria was forced to abandon her dreams of becoming a teacher due to immense pressure and settle for whatever job was available. She worked as a domestic servant in several households, often moving to different places to earn more pay and support her family.

By the time Victoria reached her mid-twenties, her siblings had grown up and pursued their ambitions, while Victoria herself was weighed down by a deep feeling of purposelessness. She longed for a fresh start, a place where she could reconnect with her authentic identity. The opportunity at Downhill emerged as an unexpected possibility. It provided her with a chance to abandon her past experiences and maybe start anew in a different way.

## Skills and Sensitive Information

Victoria possesses a unique set of skills and knowledge that would be quite advantageous in investigating the mysterious ghostly occurrences in Downhill. From a young age, Victoria exhibited an exceptional ability to perceive things that were beyond the vision of others. Her intuition was highly perceptive, often bordering on the supernatural. She had a strong ability to sense the presence of supernatural beings and had a natural knack for detecting the electromagnetic vibrations of a place, allowing her to perceive its previous occurrences and hidden secrets.

The late mother had left behind an ancient family heirloom, a little, worn-out book filled with medicinal plant formulas, traditional stories, and mysterious information about the spiritual world. Victoria assimilated the material, gaining an understanding of defensive amulets, ceremonial practices, and the signs of restless apparitions. While previously mostly theoretical, this material has given her a solid foundation for understanding the uncanny events at Downhill.

Victoria possesses a talent for sketching as well. She gained the foundational information from her father, and through practice and experience, she honed her skills. She often used her illustrations to absorb her emotions and understand the world around her. She began drawing the occurrences she encountered at Downhill, skillfully representing the spirit manifestations and the numerous complexities of the estate. Consequently, these sketches would serve as a visual record of her encounters and discoveries.

Personal incentives

Victoria's motivations for understanding the mystery of Down Hill and aiding the ghost were very personal. She had encountered substantial adversity and challenges in her previous experiences, and she felt a profound emotional connection with the melancholy that surrounded the mansion. Victoria interpreted the appearance of Juliet Ravenswood as a representation of her difficulties, and she felt a moral duty to help the spiritual entity achieve peace.

Furthermore, Victoria regarded her pursuit as a way of honoring her mother's recollections. Victoria's mother had always maintained a strong conviction in the existence of supernatural phenomena and had instilled in Victoria a deep respect for the realm of spirits. By solving the mystery and helping the ghost, Victoria felt a feeling of fulfilling a part of her mother's legacy, using the knowledge and intuition passed down to her by her mother.

Victoria's ambitions also have a pragmatic dimension.

Deciphering the mystery of the apparition would prove her worth to the staff and secure her position at Downhill. The occupation not only supplied her with financial assistance but also bestowed upon her a sense of security and, maybe, a newfound sense of belonging. Victoria perceived the house, with its concealed wisdom and history, as a place where she thought she might have a significant influence.

Ultimately, Victoria's inherent curiosity spurred her forward. As she immersed herself further in the ghost's narrative and the estate's historical background, her need to obtain knowledge intensified. As the puzzle pieces came together, Victoria's determination to understand the whole picture enabled her to face the unknown.

With the revelation of each additional clue and the acquisition of every new experience, Victoria's resolve intensified. She was not just a domestic servant carrying out her responsibilities; she was an individual seeking knowledge, healing broken spirits, and a determined woman to reveal the hidden elements of Downhill.

# Chapter Six

## Ghost's Previous Existence

Juliet Ravenswood's life was characterized by a blend of wealth, beauty, and sorrow. Juliet Winchester, being from a prestigious lineage in London, occupied the role of the youngest daughter. Her father occupied a prestigious role as a judge, while her mother was widely acknowledged and respected as a renowned socialite. Juliet was brought up in a privileged lifestyle, where she frequented extravagant social gatherings and had a first-rate education. She was recognized for her intelligence, grace, and exceptional beauty, which captivated many admirers.

Despite residing in a lavish setting, Juliet encountered challenges in her life. At the age of twelve, she was profoundly affected by the death of her older brother, Edward, as a result of an illness. Her parents, consumed by grief, withdrew from social engagements, leaving Juliet to navigate her teenage years in a family overshadowed by bereavement.

Juliet crossed paths with Lord Henry Ravenswood in her early twenties at a humanitarian event. He was a charismatic and wealthy businessperson, well-known for his ambitious nature. The pair quickly formed a deep emotional connection, and their wedding was an extravagant occasion that united two powerful families. Juliet moved to Downhill, a remarkable estate that Henry had recently commissioned.

Juliet thrived in her new abode. She actively participated in the local community, organizing charitable initiatives and providing assistance to those in need within the manor. The people greatly admired her kindness and ability to understand and share the feelings of others, which made her a highly valued and beloved person in the region. The partnership between her and Henry, while encountering challenges, was established based on reciprocal appreciation and affection.

Juliet experienced immense happiness when her son, Thomas, was born. She showered him with attention, infusing the mansion with happiness and warmth. However, the happiness was short-lived as the home rapidly turned into a place of sorrow and mystery.

Untimely demise

The circumstances surrounding Juliet's death were both sorrowful and mysterious. In the autumn of 1892, the Ravenswood family experienced a series of tragic occurrences. The tragedy began with the sudden disappearance of a young guy named Thomas. He vanished mysteriously one evening while playing in the gardens. Juliet's exhaustive quest to find him produced no outcomes, leaving her in a condition of desolation.

Juliet's health rapidly deteriorated after Thomas's abrupt departure. She became withdrawn, plagued by grief and a sense of imminent catastrophe. Despite Henry's efforts to provide comfort, she seemed to sink farther into her universe of melancholy. The staff heard rumors about Juliet's strong belief that Thomas's disappearance was linked to a curse that affected the Ravenswood family, a curse she felt powerless to break.

Juliet was found dead in her bedroom after a fateful night.

The official conclusion indicated that the individual's death was caused by a myocardial infarction, while there were ongoing discussions about possible malicious elements. There was a prevailing idea that she had dedicated herself as a result of her incapacity to handle the loss of her son. Certain individuals speculated that the curse she feared had ultimately ensnared her. The true details of her death remained mysterious, adding to the legendary stories that surrounded Downhill.

Unfinished affairs

Juliet's essence persisted in Downhill, tethered by unresolved issues and a deep sense of unfinished responsibilities. The primary cause of her anguish stemmed from the disappearance of her beloved son, Thomas. The mother's bond was strong, and her inability to find him or understand his fate left her soul disturbed.

Juliet's second source of anguish was from the curse she firmly thought had plagued the Ravenswood lineage for countless generations. She had dedicated a substantial amount of time in her life to researching the root causes of the issue and finding a resolution to overcome it, but her untimely death impeded her progress. She has a strong resolve to protect future generations from enduring the same fate.

In addition, Juliet's ability to understand and share the feelings of others, as well as her dedication, extended beyond her close family members. She had dedicated herself to helping others in need and using her position to improve society. The unfinished charitable projects and the mysteries of the estate added to her discomfort. Her otherworldly presence wandered through the hallways, longing for solace and resolution over the obligations she couldn't perform during her lifetime.

Juliet's spirit embodied a complex fusion of sorrow, fondness, and duty. Her ghostly appearances, however unsettling, were expressions of a tormented spirit in search of serenity. She reached out to Victoria, recognizing her as someone who shared similar thoughts and potentially a partner in solving the mysteries that linked her to poverty.

Victoria's investigations compassed not only uncovering the historical background of the mansion but also gradually piecing together the components of Juliet's melancholic story, drawing her nearer to the serenity she fervently longed for.

## Chapter Seven

## Allies and Adversaries

Victoria John soon discovered that she was not alone in her quest to unravel the mysteries of Down Hill. Among the staff and residents, a few individuals emerged as her allies, providing both moral support and practical assistance.

Mrs. Thompson was one of Victoria's earliest and most steadfast allies. The housekeeper, with her vast knowledge of the manor and its history, became an invaluable resource. Mrs. Thompson had been at Down Hill for over three decades and had seen many strange things. She shared her insights and guided Victoria through the labyrinthine passages of the mansion, often revealing hidden nooks and crannies that held crucial clues. Her calm demeanor and unwavering belief in Victoria's mission provided much-needed encouragement.

Peter Collins, the elderly gardener, was another key ally. His deep connection to the land and the manor's history made him a repository of local legends and untold stories.

Peter had a keen sense of the supernatural, having witnessed ghostly apparitions himself. He often accompanied Victoria on her nocturnal explorations, using his knowledge of the grounds to uncover hidden entrances and long-forgotten sites. His wisdom and gentle nature were a source of comfort and strength for Victoria.

Sarah, the young scullery maid, became an unexpected but enthusiastic supporter. Her curiosity about the ghostly happenings and her own experiences with the supernatural made her eager to help. Despite her youth, Sarah was resourceful and brave, often sneaking into restricted areas to gather information or retrieve objects of interest. Her energy and optimism were infectious, reminding Victoria of the importance of persistence and hope.

Opposing Forces

Not everyone at Down Hill was supportive of Victoria's investigation. Several characters emerged as opposing forces, each with their own reasons for hindering her progress.

Mr. Blackwood, the stern and secretive butler, was one of Victoria's main antagonists. He viewed her inquiries as a threat to the stability and reputation of the household. Mr. Blackwood was fiercely loyal to the Ravenswood family and believed that digging into the past would only bring trouble. He often obstructed Victoria's efforts, locking doors, and hiding keys, and subtly intimidating her. His enigmatic nature and unexplained absences raised suspicions about his own connections to the manor's dark history.

Lady Margaret Ravenswood, a distant relative and occasional resident of the manor, also opposed Victoria's investigation. Lady Margaret was a woman of considerable influence and prided herself on maintaining the family's social standing. She dismissed the ghost stories as foolish superstitions and viewed Victoria's actions as disruptive. Her disdain for the lower classes fueled her antagonism, and she used her authority to undermine Victoria at every turn, often spreading rumors and creating obstacles.

Dr. Albert Thompson, a frequent visitor and family friend, had his own agenda. As a physician with a keen interest in the paranormal, Dr. Thompson initially appeared supportive of Victoria's efforts. However, his motivations were far from altruistic. He sought to exploit the manor's supernatural phenomena for his own gain, hoping to publish sensational findings that would elevate his career. When Victoria began to uncover truths that contradicted his theories, Dr. Thompson became increasingly antagonistic, attempting to discredit her and manipulate the narrative to suit his ambitions.

**Unexpected Help**

Amidst the allies and adversaries, Victoria found surprising sources of assistance from unlikely characters who proved instrumental in her journey.

Mr. Simmons, the reclusive and eccentric librarian, emerged as a crucial ally. Initially perceived as aloof and indifferent, Mr. Simmons revealed a deep knowledge of the manor's extensive archives. His passion for history and keen intellect made him an invaluable partner in deciphering old manuscripts and uncovering hidden documents. Mr. Simmons's unexpected willingness to help was driven by his own quest for knowledge and a desire to see the manor's true history revealed.

Annabelle, the manor's resident cat, became an unlikely but indispensable companion. The sleek, black feline had a knack for appearing at opportune moments, often leading Victoria to hidden passages or concealed objects. Annabelle's seemingly supernatural awareness of the mansion's secrets hinted at her own mysterious connection to the manor's past. Victoria came to trust Annabelle's instincts, following her lead on numerous occasions to uncover vital clues.

Father Benedict, the local parish priest, provided spiritual and emotional support. Though he was skeptical of the supernatural, Father Benedict recognized the sincerity of Victoria's quest and offered guidance and counsel. His deep sense of morality and justice aligned with Victoria's determination to help the restless spirits. Father Benedict's unexpected empathy and wisdom offered Victoria a grounding perspective and bolstered her resolve to continue her investigation.

Through the support of these diverse and unexpected allies, Victoria John's journey at Down Hill became a collaborative effort. Each ally brought unique strengths and insights, helping her navigate the complexities of the mansion's dark history. Together, they faced the opposing forces and unraveled the mysteries that bound the restless spirits, inching closer to bringing peace to the haunted halls of Down Hill.

# Chapter Eight

## The Haunting Intensifies

As the days turned into weeks, the supernatural activity within Down Hill intensified dramatically. What began as subtle disturbances—like flickering lights and cold drafts—quickly escalated into full-blown hauntings that affected everyone in the mansion. Victoria noticed the change almost immediately. The air grew heavier with an oppressive energy, and the manor's shadows seemed to deepen and move with a life of their own.

One night, as Victoria was preparing for bed, she heard a series of loud, inexplicable bangs coming from the east wing. Rushing to investigate, she found furniture overturned and paintings askew, as if an unseen force had ransacked the rooms in a fit of rage. The other staff members reported similar experiences: Mrs. Thompson found the kitchen in disarray every morning, with pots and pans strewn about, while Peter Collins discovered the garden tools mysteriously relocated and damaged.

The hauntings became more personal and invasive. Victoria awoke several times to find her belongings moved or missing, only to reappear in bizarre locations. She often felt a chilling presence hovering near her, and on more than one occasion, she caught glimpses of ghostly figures out of the corner of her eye. The once sporadic encounters with Juliet's spirit now became almost nightly events, with the ghost appearing at the foot of Victoria's bed, her eyes filled with a desperate plea for help.

**Dangerous Encounters**

With the increased activity came more dangerous encounters. One evening, as Victoria explored a rarely used corridor in the west wing, she was confronted by a malevolent spirit she had never seen before. This ghost, a tall, shadowy figure with glowing red eyes, exuded a menacing aura. As Victoria tried to back away, the spirit lunged at her, knocking her to the ground and leaving her with deep scratches on her arms. It took every ounce of her willpower to escape and make it back to her room.

Others in the household were not spared from these sinister forces. Mrs. Thompson was nearly pushed down a flight of stairs by an unseen hand, narrowly catching herself on the banister. Sarah experienced terrifying episodes where she felt hands grasping at her in the darkness, leaving her paralyzed with fear. Even the usually stoic Mr. Blackwood began to exhibit signs of distress, his demeanor growing increasingly anxious and erratic.

The most harrowing encounter occurred one stormy night when Victoria, Peter Collins, and Sarah ventured into the cellar in search of more clues. As they descended into the damp, musty darkness, they were confronted by a swirling vortex of ghostly apparitions. The spirits shrieked and howled, their faces twisted in agony. The trio barely escaped with their lives, driven back by the sheer malevolence emanating from the cellar.

**Seeking Protection**

Realizing that the hauntings were becoming increasingly dangerous, Victoria and her allies knew they had to take steps to protect themselves and the other residents of Down Hill. Drawing on her mother's teachings and the knowledge from her heirloom book, Victoria devised several protective measures.

Victoria began by creating protective charms and amulets for everyone in the household. Using herbs, crystals, and symbols from the old book, she crafted talismans designed to ward off malevolent spirits. Each member of the staff wore these amulets, hoping they would provide some measure of safety against the growing threat.

In addition to the amulets, Victoria and Mrs. Thompson conducted cleansing rituals throughout the mansion. They burned sage and other purifying herbs, reciting prayers and incantations meant to banish negative energy. These rituals seemed to have a temporary calming effect, but the malevolent spirits always returned, seemingly more enraged than before.

Seeking more permanent solutions, Victoria turned to Father Benedict for spiritual guidance. He performed a series of blessings and exorcisms in the most haunted areas of the manor. His presence and rituals provided a brief respite from the hauntings, giving the residents a much-needed sense of hope and protection. Father Benedict also taught Victoria and the others prayers and protective rituals to perform on their own, empowering them to stand against the supernatural forces.

Despite these efforts, Victoria knew that these measures were only temporary fixes. The hauntings would not cease until the root cause—the unresolved issues tethering the spirits to the mansion—was addressed. Victoria's resolve to uncover the truth and help the restless spirits find peace grew stronger with each passing day. She continued her investigation with renewed determination, driven by the need to protect herself and her newfound friends from the escalating horrors of Down Hill.

Victoria's journey was fraught with danger, but she was not alone. With the support of her allies and the protective measures they put in place, she faced the escalating hauntings head-on, determined to bring an end to the mansion's dark legacy. The intensifying supernatural activity only fueled her determination to uncover the truth and bring peace to the restless spirits of Down Hill.

# Chapter Nine

## Discovering The Truth

Victoria John's determination to uncover the truth about the haunting of Down Hill grew stronger with each passing day. The intense supernatural activity had brought a renewed sense of urgency to her mission. Drawing on the clues she had gathered, Victoria began to piece together the fragments of the past, constructing a narrative that connected the ghost of Juliet Ravenswood to the mysterious events that plagued the mansion.

Her meticulous investigations led her to recognize patterns in the hauntings, connecting them to specific locations and times. Each encounter with Juliet's spirit seemed to hint at certain events or periods in the mansion's history. Victoria carefully documented every detail, creating a timeline that aligned with the major incidents and sightings. Her sketches, notes, and observations gradually formed a cohesive picture of Juliet's tragic life and untimely death.

Victoria's conversations with her allies were also crucial. Mrs. Thompson's extensive knowledge of the manor's history, Peter Collins's local legends, and Sarah's observations of the supernatural all contributed to Victoria's understanding. Together, they speculated about the possible connections between the Ravenswood curse, Juliet's death, and the disappearance of her son, Thomas.

## Hidden Documents

One stormy afternoon, as Victoria was sorting through old trunks in the attic, she made a remarkable discovery. Among the dusty relics and forgotten memorabilia, she found a hidden compartment in an ornate chest. Inside were a bundle of letters and a weathered journal. The letters were addressed to Juliet Ravenswood and dated back to the months before her death. They were from a mysterious correspondent, urging Juliet to take drastic measures to protect her family from an ancient curse.

The journal, written in Juliet's own hand, provided a firsthand account of her final days. It detailed her growing fears for her son, her belief in the family curse, and her desperate attempts to uncover its origins. Juliet's words conveyed her anguish and determination, offering a poignant glimpse into her psyche. She described secret meetings with a local occultist who claimed to have knowledge of the curse and offered potential solutions.

Among the letters was a cryptic map, marked with symbols and annotations that seemed to point to hidden locations within the manor. Victoria felt a surge of excitement as she realized these documents held the key to understanding the full extent of Juliet's struggle and the true nature of the curse.

**Confronting the Past**

Armed with this new information, Victoria knew she had to confront those who had played a role in Juliet's tragic story. Her first stop was to speak with Mr. Blackwood. Despite his antagonistic behavior, Victoria suspected he knew more than he had let on. She found him in his office, going through old ledgers. With the hidden documents in hand, she confronted him, demanding the truth.

At first, Mr. Blackwood was reluctant to speak, but the sight of Juliet's journal and the urgency in Victoria's voice broke through his defenses. He admitted that he had been aware of the family curse and Juliet's efforts to combat it. He had been sworn to secrecy by Lord Henry Ravenswood, who feared that public knowledge of the curse would ruin the family's reputation. Mr. Blackwood revealed that he had been instructed to destroy any evidence related to the curse but had hidden some documents out of a sense of loyalty to Juliet.

Next, Victoria sought out Lady Margaret Ravenswood. Though initially dismissive, Lady Margaret's demeanor changed when Victoria presented the letters and journal. Confronted with undeniable evidence, she reluctantly shared what she knew. Lady Margaret revealed that the Ravenswood family had been plagued by misfortune for generations, always whispered to be the result of a curse.

She had dismissed Juliet's fears as hysteria at the time, but now regretted her lack of support.

Victoria also visited Dr. Albert Thompson, the physician with a hidden agenda. She cornered him in the library, showing him the journal and demanding his cooperation. Realizing that Victoria had uncovered significant truths, Dr. Thompson confessed that he had indeed manipulated events to further his own career. He had exploited Juliet's desperation, providing her with dubious rituals and false hope in exchange for her trust and access to her resources.

With these confrontations, Victoria gathered the final pieces of the puzzle. She now understood that Juliet's untimely death and Thomas's disappearance were intrinsically linked to the family curse and the dark secrets buried within the manor's walls. The hidden documents, combined with the testimonies of those involved, revealed a tale of love, loss, and a desperate struggle against malevolent forces.

Victoria's journey was far from over, but she now had a clearer path forward. She was determined to honor Juliet's memory by continuing her fight against the curse and finding a way to bring peace to the restless spirits of Down Hill. Armed with the truth and the support of her allies, Victoria prepared to delve deeper into the mansion's darkest secrets, ready to face whatever challenges lay ahead.

# Chapter Ten

## The Ghost Request

### Communicating with the Ghost

The atmosphere in Down Hill had grown more tense and eerie, with supernatural events occurring more frequently and with greater intensity. Amidst this heightened activity, Victoria John became acutely aware of Juliet Ravenswood's presence. One night, as Victoria sat by the dim light of her lantern, the air grew cold, and a whispering wind seemed to sweep through her room. The ghost of Juliet appeared, more solid and tangible than ever before, her ethereal form shimmering in the faint glow.

Juliet's expression was a mixture of sorrow and urgency. Through a series of haunting gestures and soft, otherworldly murmurs, she began to communicate her needs to Victoria. Juliet's message was clear: she needed Victoria's help to find peace. Her eyes, filled with a pleading intensity, conveyed the depth of her anguish and the importance of the task she was entrusting to Victoria.

Using a combination of gestures and images that appeared in Victoria's mind, Juliet revealed the nature of her request. She needed Victoria to find her son, Thomas, whose disappearance had been the catalyst for her eternal unrest. Juliet believed that Thomas was still somewhere within the grounds of Down Hill, lost and waiting to be found. The search for Thomas was not just about locating his physical form but also uncovering the truth about what had happened to him.

## A Difficult Task

The task before Victoria was daunting. She knew that finding Thomas would require delving deeper into the darkest corners of the manor, places where the malevolent spirits held the strongest sway. She would need to explore areas that had been untouched for decades, risking encounters with the most dangerous entities in the mansion

She needed to piece together the fragmented clues that might lead her to Thomas, clues hidden within the cryptic documents, old maps, and Juliet's journal.

Victoria's first step was to revisit the hidden locations marked on the cryptic map she had found among Juliet's letters. With Peter Collins and Sarah by her side, she ventured into the forgotten basements, the concealed rooms, and the secret passages of Down Hill. Each exploration brought them closer to understanding the layout and secrets of the mansion, but the dangers they faced also increased. Malevolent spirits seemed determined to thwart their progress, manifesting as shadowy figures and poltergeist activity that threatened their safety.

Despite these challenges, Victoria persevered. Her determination to help Juliet find peace and to uncover the truth about Thomas fueled her courage. She discovered hidden artifacts—an old locket with Thomas's picture, a torn piece of his clothing, and an ancient family tree that hinted at the curse's origins. These items, imbued with the emotional resonance of the past, provided crucial clues and led Victoria to the final, most perilous part of her journey.

## Moral Dilemmas

As Victoria delved deeper into the mystery, she faced several moral and ethical dilemmas. One of the most pressing was whether to share her findings with the rest of the household. While some, like Mrs. Thompson and Father Benedict, were supportive, others, particularly Mr. Blackwood and Lady Margaret, were likely to react with fear or hostility. Victoria had to weigh the potential benefits of their help against the risk of further conflict and disruption within the already tense household.

Another moral dilemma arose when Victoria discovered that the family curse might not only be a supernatural affliction but also tied to the actions of past Ravenswood family members. Uncovering the truth about Thomas's disappearance and the curse involved revealing dark secrets that some might prefer remained hidden. Victoria had to decide whether to expose these truths, knowing it could tarnish the family's legacy and bring shame to the living Ravenswoods.

The most difficult ethical challenge came when Victoria learned that breaking the curse and helping Juliet find peace might require a significant sacrifice. According to the occult texts and the occultist's notes found in Juliet's journal, a ritual involving a living descendant of the Ravenswood family might be necessary to sever the ties binding the spirits to the mansion. This meant asking someone—perhaps even Lady Margaret or another family member—to risk their life or well-being for the sake of the spirits.

Victoria struggled with these moral questions, seeking counsel from Father Benedict, who emphasized the importance of compassion, truth, and the greater good. Ultimately, Victoria realized that helping Juliet and Thomas and freeing the mansion from its curse, was a righteous cause that could bring peace to the tormented spirits and the living alike.

With a heavy heart and unwavering resolve, Victoria prepared to fulfill Juliet's request. She gathered her allies, armed herself with the knowledge and artifacts she had collected, and steeled herself for the final confrontation with the forces that held Down Hill in their dark grip. The path ahead was fraught with danger and moral complexity, but Victoria knew that she had to see it through to the end, for the sake of Juliet, Thomas, and all who had suffered within the haunted halls of Down Hill.

# Chapter Eleven

## The Supernatural Ally

### A New Presence

The relentless haunting of Downhill continued to escalate, with Victoria John and her allies feeling the weight of their task more heavily each day. Amidst the chaos and fear, a new presence made itself known. This new supernatural entity was different from the malevolent spirits that plagued the manor—it was benevolent and seemed to exude a calming, protective energy.

One night, as Victoria sat in her room, poring over Juliet's journal and the cryptic map, she felt a sudden warmth enveloping her. The air shimmered, and a soft glow filled the room. Before her appeared a translucent figure of a middle-aged woman with kind eyes and a serene expression. She introduced herself as Lois, a former resident of the manor from the late 19th century. Lois explained that she had once been a governess in the household, and her spirit had remained bound to the manor, not out of malice, but out of a desire to protect and guide those in need.

Lois's presence was immediately comforting. Unlike the other spirits, she did not instill fear or dread. Instead, she radiated a sense of peace and wisdom. Victoria felt an instant connection to her, sensing that Lois was a true ally in her quest to uncover the truth and bring peace to Juliet's restless spirit.

**Guidance and Wisdom**

Lois proved to be an invaluable source of guidance and knowledge. She shared her own experiences and observations from her time in the manor, providing historical context and filling in gaps that the other documents and artifacts could not. Lois had witnessed the early manifestations of the curse and had spent her life trying to protect the Ravenswood children from its effects. Her insights into the family's history and the curse were profound.

One of Lois's most crucial pieces of advice was about the hidden locations within the manor. She guided Victoria to a concealed library that even Mrs. Thompson had not known existed. The library contained books and manuscripts detailing the Ravenswood lineage, occult practices, and the curse's origins. Lois helped Victoria decipher these texts, revealing the ancient rituals and symbols necessary to break the curse.

Lois also taught Victoria protective charms and rituals to ward off the malevolent spirits. These methods proved more effective than the ones Victoria had been using, providing a stronger defense against the escalating supernatural attacks. With Lois's guidance, Victoria felt more confident and equipped to face the challenges ahead.

**Strengthening Bonds**

As Victoria and Lois worked together, their bond grew stronger. Victoria found herself confiding in Lois, sharing her fears, doubts, and hopes. Lois, in turn, offered not only practical advice but also emotional support. She became a mentor and a friend, someone Victoria could rely on in the darkest moments.

Their relationship deepened as they spent more time together. Lois's calm demeanor and unwavering support provided Victoria with a sense of stability amidst the chaos. Victoria began to understand Lois's motivations and the deep care she had for the Ravenswood family, which mirrored Victoria's own growing attachment to the manor and its inhabitants.

One poignant moment in their bond came when Lois shared her own tragic story. She had fallen in love with one of the Ravenswood sons, but their love was forbidden due to their social differences. Lois had died under mysterious circumstances, which she now believed were linked to the curse. Her spirit remained bound to the manor, not out of unfinished business for herself, but out of a desire to protect those she had cared for in life.

This revelation deepened Victoria's resolve to break the curse and bring peace to the spirits trapped within the manor. She realized that her mission was not just about solving a mystery, but about honoring the lives and loves of those who had come before her. Lois's story added a personal dimension to Victoria's quest, making it all the more important to succeed.

Through their growing bond, Victoria and Lois formed a powerful partnership. Lois's wisdom and Victoria's determination complemented each other, creating a force strong enough to stand against the malevolent spirits and the curse. Together, they continued their search for Thomas and the ultimate solution to the haunting, each step bringing them closer to uncovering the final pieces of the puzzle.

In the end, Victoria knew that with Lois by her side, she had the strength and support she needed to face whatever lay ahead. Their bond was a testament to the power of compassion, understanding, and the enduring connections that transcended even death. As they prepared for the final stages of their journey, Victoria felt a renewed sense of hope and purpose, ready to confront the darkness with the light of their shared determination.

# Chapter Twelve

## The Final Puzzle

### Unlocking Secrets

The atmosphere in Down Hill had reached a fever pitch of supernatural activity, but Victoria John remained resolute. With Lois's guidance and the support of her allies, she felt prepared to uncover the final secrets needed to solve the mystery and free Juliet's tormented spirit. The discovery of the hidden library had been a turning point, providing critical information about the Ravenswood curse and the ancient rituals necessary to break it.

Victoria spent countless hours poring over the old manuscripts, deciphering the arcane symbols and instructions. She meticulously mapped out the manor's layout, cross-referencing it with the cryptic map she had found. Lois pointed her toward a specific area of the mansion: the family crypt. It was there, according to the texts, that the heart of the curse lay buried, along with the remains of the Ravenswood ancestors who had first invoked it.

Determined to confront the source of the curse, Victoria gathered her allies—Peter Collins, Mrs. Thompson, Sarah, and Father Benedict. Each of them played a crucial role in the upcoming confrontation. Peter's knowledge of the manor's secret passages, Mrs. Thompson's historical insights, Sarah's courage, and Father Benedict's spiritual strength were all vital.

**Ancient Rituals**

As night fell, the group made their way to the family crypt, armed with the artifacts, protective charms, and instructions for the ancient ritual. The crypt was a cold, foreboding place, filled with the echoes of the past and the weight of countless tragedies. Candles flickered in the dark, casting eerie shadows on the stone walls adorned with the names of the departed Ravenswood ancestors.

Victoria took a deep breath and began the ritual, following the precise steps outlined in the manuscripts. She placed the artifacts—Juliet's locket, Thomas's torn clothing, and the ancient family tree—on an altar she had constructed in the center of the crypt. The group formed a protective circle around her, each holding a candle and reciting the incantations Lois had taught them.

As Victoria chanted the ancient words, the air grew thick with a palpable energy. The candles' flames danced wildly, and the ground beneath them trembled. A low, ominous hum filled the crypt, resonating with the power of the ritual. Victoria felt a surge of strength and determination, fueled by the presence of her allies and the guidance of Lois.

Suddenly, a blinding light erupted from the altar, illuminating the entire crypt. The malevolent spirits that had tormented the manor appeared, drawn to the powerful ritual. They howled and writhed, their forms twisted in anguish. But the protective circle held strong, and the spirits could not breach it.

Victoria continued the incantation, her voice unwavering. She invoked the names of the Ravenswood ancestors, calling upon them to release their hold on the present and allow Juliet's spirit to find peace. The ritual required a final offering—an act of sacrifice. With a steady hand, Victoria drew a small vial of her blood and poured it onto the altar, sealing the incantation with her life force.

## The Moment of Truth

As the last words of the incantation left her lips, the crypt fell silent. The blinding light dimmed, revealing Juliet's ghost standing before the altar, her form more solid and serene than ever before. She gazed at Victoria with gratitude and sorrow, her eyes filled with a sense of release.

In that pivotal moment, the air seemed to crackle with a sense of finality. The malevolent spirits began to dissipate, their howls turning into whispers and then silence. The oppressive weight that had hung over Down Hill for generations lifted, replaced by a profound sense of peace.

Juliet approached Victoria, her ghostly hand reaching out to touch her cheek. "Thank you," she whispered, her voice a soft echo. "You have freed me and my son."

As Juliet's spirit began to fade, a young boy's figure appeared beside her—Thomas. He smiled at Victoria, his eyes filled with the innocence of a child finally at peace. Together, they turned and walked into the light, their forms merging with the radiance that now filled the crypt.

Victoria felt tears stream down her face, a mixture of relief, joy, and sorrow. She had fulfilled her promise to Juliet and Thomas, bringing an end to their suffering and the curse that had plagued the Ravenswood family. The ancient rituals, the sacrifices, and the unwavering support of her allies had culminated in this moment of truth.

The group stood in silence, each reflecting on the profound events they had just witnessed. The crypt, once a place of darkness and despair, now felt like a sacred space, filled with the lingering presence of peace and resolution.

As they left the crypt, Victoria knew that Down Hill would never be the same. The hauntings had ceased, and the spirits had found their rest. She felt a deep sense of accomplishment and a renewed purpose. Her journey had transformed her, forging bonds of friendship and uncovering truths that would resonate for generations to come.

Victoria John had faced the darkness and emerged victorious, bringing light and peace to Down Hill and its troubled history.

## Chapter Thirteen

### The Climax

The peace following the ritual in the crypt was short-lived. While Juliet and Thomas's spirits had found rest, a deeper, more malevolent force stirred within the bowels of Down Hill. Victoria John sensed it in the oppressive air and the whispering shadows that clung to the corners of every room. This was the true source of the curse, a malevolent entity that had bound itself to the Ravenswood lineage for centuries.

The final confrontation began on a stormy night, as thunder rumbled and lightning illuminated the manor's ancient walls. Victoria had prepared for this moment, gathering her allies and arming herself with the knowledge and tools she had accumulated. Lois's spirit remained by her side, offering support and guidance.

The group made their way to the grand ballroom, a vast, opulent space now shrouded in darkness and foreboding energy. Victoria knew that this was the heart of the manor, where the malevolent force had the strongest hold. As they entered, the temperature dropped, and an eerie silence enveloped them. The chandeliers flickered, casting ghostly shadows that seemed to move of their own accord.

Suddenly, the room erupted in chaos. The malevolent entity manifested as a swirling vortex of darkness and rage, its form ever-shifting and filled with the faces of those it had tormented. It spoke in a cacophony of voices, accusing and mocking Victoria and her allies.

"You think you can free them?" it hissed. "You are nothing but a speck, a fleeting breath in the winds of time. I am eternal. I am the curse that binds this family."

**Life or Death**

The confrontation escalated quickly, with the malevolent entity lashing out in fury. Victoria and her allies were thrown back by a powerful force, the very ground beneath them trembling. Victoria struggled to her feet, her heart pounding. She knew this was a life-or-death situation, and the stakes had never been higher.

Father Benedict stepped forward, reciting a powerful exorcism prayer. His voice rang out, strong and unwavering, as he held a crucifix aloft. The entity recoiled, its form writhing in agony. Victoria joined in, chanting the incantations she had learned, while Sarah and Mrs. Thompson used the protective charms to shield the group from the entity's attacks.

The battle was intense, with the entity summoning shadowy tendrils and ghostly apparitions to assail them. Peter Collins fought bravely, using his knowledge of the manor's layout to outmaneuver the spectral forces. Lois's spirit provided crucial guidance, directing Victoria to the focal point of the entity's power—a blackened, ancient altar hidden beneath the ballroom's floor.

Victoria realized that to defeat the entity, she needed to destroy this altar. With Lois's help, she located it and began the arduous task of dismantling it. The entity, sensing its impending doom, intensified its attacks, focusing its wrath on Victoria. Shadows closed in around her, the cold seeping into her bones as the entity tried to crush her spirit.

In a desperate moment, Victoria remembered the vial of her blood she had used in the previous ritual. She took it out, knowing that another sacrifice might be needed. Summoning all her courage, she poured the remaining blood onto the altar, invoking the protective spirits of Juliet and Thomas to aid her.

## Resolution of the Haunting

The effect was immediate and profound. A blinding light erupted from the altar, illuminating the entire ballroom. The malevolent entity shrieked, its form dissolving in the pure, radiant energy. The faces within the vortex faded away, their tormented expressions transforming into ones of relief and peace.

As the light subsided, the ballroom returned to its former state, the oppressive atmosphere lifted. The malevolent entity was gone, its hold on the manor broken. Victoria and her allies stood in stunned silence, the realization of their victory slowly sinking in.

Lois's spirit appeared before them, her face serene and filled with gratitude. "You have done it, Victoria," she said softly. "You have freed this house and its souls."

Victoria felt a wave of relief and exhaustion wash over her. The haunting of Down Hill had finally been resolved. The spirits trapped within its walls were at peace, and the curse that had plagued the Ravenswood family for generations was lifted.

The group made their way out of the ballroom, the dawn's first light breaking through the storm clouds. Victoria looked back at the manor, its grandeur now restored, and felt a sense of fulfillment and closure. She had faced the ultimate confrontation, risked her life, and emerged victorious.

Down Hill was no longer a place of fear and darkness. It had been reclaimed, its halls echoing with the promise of new beginnings. Victoria knew that while her journey had been fraught with danger and uncertainty, it had also brought her strength, friendship, and a deeper understanding of herself and the world beyond.

As they stepped into the fresh morning air, Victoria took a deep breath, ready to embrace whatever the future held. The haunting was over, but the story of Down Hill and its brave housemaid would be remembered for generations to come.

# Chapter Fourteen

## Aftermath

### The Ghost's Departure

As the first rays of dawn illuminated Down Hill, the once-foreboding atmosphere had been replaced by a serene calm. Victoria John stood in the grand ballroom, the site of their ultimate confrontation with the malevolent entity. The room was now bathed in soft, warm light, and the oppressive shadows had dissipated.

Juliet's ghost appeared one last time, her form radiant and peaceful. She approached Victoria, her eyes filled with gratitude. "Thank you," she whispered. "You have freed us. I can now find peace."

Victoria felt a lump in her throat as she nodded. "You deserve it, Juliet. You and Thomas both."

The ghost of young Thomas appeared beside his mother, smiling at Victoria with a childlike innocence. He reached out to touch her hand, his ethereal fingers passing through hers, leaving a sensation of warmth and comfort. Together, Juliet and Thomas began to fade, their spirits dissolving into the morning light. Victoria watched them go, tears streaming down her face, feeling a mixture of sadness and relief. Their departure marked the end of a long and painful chapter for the Ravenswood family, and Victoria couldn't help but feel deeply moved by their release.

## Changes in the Mansion

In the days following the resolution of the haunting, Down Hill transformed. The once eerie and neglected mansion seemed to come alive as if the very walls were shedding the years of sorrow and despair. The oppressive cold lifted, replaced by a welcoming warmth. Sunlight streamed through the large windows, casting golden hues on the polished wooden floors and intricate tapestries.

The staff and residents of the manor also began to change. Mrs. Thompson, once stern and guarded, seemed to soften, her demeanor becoming more open and kind. She shared stories of the manor's past, recounting tales of happier times and the legacy of the Ravenswood family. Peter Collins, who had always been pragmatic and reserved, found a new sense of purpose in restoring the manor to its former glory. His laughter and good-natured teasing became more frequent, lightening the mood of those around him.

Lady Margaret, the last of the Ravenswood line, appeared rejuvenated. The weight of the curse lifted, she seemed to stand taller, her eyes bright with a new determination to honor her family's history while creating a more hopeful future. She began to host gatherings and events, inviting the local community to share in the manor's restored beauty and history.

Father Benedict continued to provide spiritual support, his presence a comforting constant. He helped organize a memorial for the spirits who had found peace, a ceremony that brought closure to the household and honored the lives of Juliet, Thomas, and the other restless souls.

## Personal Growth

For Victoria, the experience had been transformative. Reflecting on her journey, she realized how much she had grown since her arrival at Down Hill. The timid, uncertain young woman who had taken the job as a housemaid was now a confident, courageous individual who had faced the supernatural and emerged victorious.

Victoria's backstory of personal loss and the need for a fresh start had initially driven her to take the job at the manor. She had carried with her the weight of her own unresolved past, but through her interactions with Juliet and the other spirits, she had found a way to confront her own fears and insecurities. She had learned the importance of empathy, resilience, and the strength that comes from forming deep connections with others.

The friendships she had forged with the manor's staff and residents became an integral part of her life. Sarah, in particular, had become like a sister to her, their bond strengthened through shared trials and triumphs. Victoria also found herself growing closer to Peter, their mutual respect and camaraderie blossoming into a deeper affection.

Lois's spirit, too, had played a crucial role in Victoria's personal growth. Lois's guidance and support had not only helped Victoria navigate the mysteries of the manor but also taught her valuable lessons about sacrifice, love, and the enduring power of the human spirit.

As Victoria stood in the restored ballroom, she felt a profound sense of fulfillment. She had not only helped free the spirits trapped in the manor but had also found a sense of peace and purpose for herself. The haunting had tested her in ways she had never imagined, but it had also given her the strength to move forward with confidence and hope.

Victoria decided to stay at Down Hill, not as a housemaid, but as a steward of its history and a guardian of its newfound peace. She and Lady Margaret worked together to ensure that the manor remained a place of beauty and remembrance, where the past was honored, and the future was embraced with open arms.

The story of Victoria John and Down Hill would be remembered for generations, a tale of courage, compassion, and the enduring power of love to overcome even the darkest of curses.

## Chapter Fifteen

### A New Beginning

**Moving Forward**

With the haunting behind her and the malevolent entity defeated, Victoria John felt a renewed sense of purpose and clarity. Downhill was no longer a place of fear and sorrow but a beacon of hope and renewal. Victoria had decided to stay on at the manor, not as a housemaid, but as a caretaker and curator of its rich history.

She and Lady Margaret worked closely together, planning restorations and events that would celebrate the manor's storied past while inviting the community to share in its new chapter. Victoria took on the role of historian and storyteller, ensuring that the tales of the Ravenswood family and the many souls who had passed through its halls were preserved and honored.

Peter Collins continued to be an invaluable ally, his practical skills and deep connection to the manor making him a natural leader in the restoration efforts. He and

Victoria grew even closer, their bond solidified by their shared experiences and mutual respect. Their relationship, once marked by professional distance, blossomed into a deep and affectionate partnership.

Victoria also began to reach out to the local community, inviting historians, paranormal researchers, and curious visitors to explore Down Hill. She organized tours and lectures, sharing the manor's history and the remarkable story of its haunting and subsequent liberation. The manor became a place of learning and discovery, a testament to the resilience of its inhabitants.

Unfinished Stories

Despite the peace that now enveloped Down Hill, Victoria knew that some mysteries remained unsolved. The hidden library had revealed many secrets, but there were still cryptic passages and untranslated symbols that hinted at deeper, more ancient forces at play. Victoria couldn't shake the feeling that the manor still held more stories waiting to be uncovered.

One particular manuscript, found in the hidden library, spoke of a long-lost Ravenswood heir who had disappeared under mysterious circumstances. The manuscript hinted at a secret lineage and a potential treasure buried somewhere on the grounds. Victoria felt a spark of excitement at the thought of another mystery to solve, and she made a mental note to investigate further.

Additionally, there were still whispers of other supernatural occurrences in the nearby village and surrounding areas. Local legends spoke of haunted woods and cursed artifacts, suggesting that the malevolent force they had defeated might not be the only dark presence in the region. Victoria felt a pull toward these unexplored mysteries, sensing that her journey as a paranormal investigator was far from over.

A Final Farewell

One evening, as the sun set over Down Hill, casting a golden glow over its restored façade, Victoria stood on the balcony, reflecting on her journey. The manor, once a place of dread, now stood as a monument to the power of courage and compassion. The gardens below were blooming, the rooms within filled with laughter and light, and the ghosts of the past finally at peace.

Lois's spirit appeared beside her, a serene and comforting presence. "You have done well, Victoria," she said, her voice a gentle echo in the evening air. "This place is truly alive again, thanks to you."

Victoria smiled, feeling a deep sense of fulfillment. "I couldn't have done it without you, Lois. Or without everyone else who stood by me."

Lois nodded, her form beginning to fade as the last rays of sunlight dipped below the horizon. "Remember, Victoria, the journey never truly ends. There are always new stories to uncover, new mysteries to solve. Stay curious, stay brave."

As Lois's spirit vanished, Victoria felt a renewed determination. She knew that her time at Down Hill was just the beginning of a larger adventure. There were still many stories to tell, many secrets to uncover, and she was ready to face whatever came next with the same courage and resolve that had seen her through the darkest times.

With a final glance at the manor, Victoria turned and walked back inside, her heart full of hope and excitement for the future. She knew that whatever lay ahead, she was ready to embrace it with open arms.

And so, the story of Victoria John and Down Hill concluded with a sense of completion and anticipation. The haunting was over, but the echoes of its history would continue to inspire and intrigue. Victoria's journey had transformed her, and she was now poised to explore new horizons, guided by the lessons of the past and the promise of the future.

As the night settled over Down Hill, a sense of peace enveloped the ancient house, and a new beginning dawned, filled with endless possibilities and untold stories waiting to be discovered.